P9-DER-096

MOBS IN THE MINE

MOBS IN THE MINE

AN UNOFFICIAL MINETRAPPED ADVENTURE, #2

Winter Morgan

Sky Pony Press
New York

This book is not authorized or sponsored
by Microsoft Corp., Mojang AB, Notch
Development AB or Scholastic Inc., or
any other person or entity owning or
controlling rights in the Minecraft name,
trademark, or copyrights.

Copyright © 2016 by Hollan Publishing, Inc.

Minecraft® is a registered trademark of Notch Development AB.

The Minecraft game is copyright © Mojang AB.

This book is not authorized or sponsored by Microsoft Corp., Mojang
AB, Notch Development AB or Scholastic Inc., or any other person or
entity owning or controlling rights in the Minecraft name, trademark, or
copyrights.

All rights reserved. No part of this book may be reproduced in any manner
without the express written consent of the publisher, except in the case of
brief excerpts in critical reviews or articles. All inquiries should be addressed
to Sky Pony Press, 307 West 36th Street, 11th Floor, New York, NY 10018.

Sky Pony Press books may be purchased in bulk at special discounts for sales
promotion, corporate gifts, fund-raising, or educational purposes. Special
editions can also be created to specifications. For details, contact the Special
Sales Department, Sky Pony Press, 307 West 36th Street, 11th Floor,
New York, NY 10018 or info@skyhorsepublishing.com.

Sky Pony® is a registered trademark of Skyhorse Publishing, Inc.®,
a Delaware corporation.

Minecraft® is a registered trademark of Notch Development AB.
The Minecraft game is copyright © Mojang AB.

Visit our website at www.skyponypress.com.

10 9 8 7 6 5 4 3 2 1

Library of Congress Cataloging-in-Publication Data is available on file.

Cover design by Brian Peterson
Cover photo by Megan Miller

Print ISBN: 978-1-5107-0598-2
Ebook ISBN: 978-1-5107-0608-8

Printed in Canada

TABLE OF CONTENTS

MOBS IN THE MINE

1
RUMORS

"It can't be true," Lily dismissed her friend's comment. "Everyone knows all of the players on this server are trapped in the Overworld."

"No," Simon argued. "I was in town, and a player said they spotted a man wearing a green jumpsuit, just like the Prismarines."

"Nobody's heard from Brett, Greta, or any of the Prismarines in ages," Lily protested.

"But I saw him." Simon was annoyed at Lily. She didn't seem to believe him.

"That was probably just a coincidence. Maybe they were just dressed the same way?"

"No," Simon remarked. "I'm sure he was one of the Prismarines."

"Well, where is he?" questioned Lily.

"I'm not sure," said Simon. "Maybe he was captured by Mr. Anarchy."

"That's awful," said Michael.

"That would be just like Mr. Anarchy," Lily said.

"I'm sure that terrible griefer is at home dreaming up a new plot to destroy Lisimi Village." Michael paced as he spoke.

"We have to go find the man in the green jumpsuit and help him," added Simon.

Lily paused. "I don't know if we should. I think this is a trap."

"Why?" asked Simon.

"I think the man in the green jumpsuit is actually a blue griefer working for Mr. Anarchy, and he is trying to trick us into traveling to the dangerous jungle biome, where we will be trapped and imprisoned," Lily theorized.

A group of townspeople approached the trio, and Lily spotted her friend, Warren, in the crowd.

Warren raced to the front of the crowd and said, "We heard rumors that one of the Prismarines has returned to the server."

Lily asked, "Who told you that?"

Warren replied, "I know Juan the Butcher saw him."

The townspeople called out names of various people who also spotted the man in the green jumpsuit.

"I think we are being tricked. It could be one of Mr. Anarchy's griefers. Maybe Mr. Anarchy made him change his skin so he would look like a Prismarine." Lily was convinced that the man in the green jumpsuit was an imposter.

"There's only one way we can find out," said Warren. "We will have to go to the jungle biome."

"But what if it's a trap?" Lily called out again.

The debate was over when a townsperson shouted, "I see him! He hasn't left."

The trio and the townspeople ran toward the man in the green jumpsuit, but when they approached him, he splashed a potion of invisibility on himself and disappeared.

"I told you I didn't trust him," Lily said.

"This isn't good." Michael was worried. "We've had a very long period of peace in which we were able to plot ways to return home. I think now Mr. Anarchy is back, and he's going to cause serious trouble."

Everyone agreed.

"What should we do?" asked Simon.

A loud roar boomed through their small village.

"He's unleashed the Ender Dragon!" Lily's voice shook.

"I guess he wants to initiate a battle." Simon grabbed a bow and arrow from his inventory and aimed at the Ender Dragon.

Lily held a snowball and threw it at the powerful beast as it flew through the sky. The scaly wings from the dragon crushed an entire block of stores in the village.

"My butcher shop!" Juan called out.

Lily slammed a snowball into the dragon's side. It lost hearts. "Everyone, shoot whatever you can at the dragon," she yelled.

Arrows and snowballs flew through the air, but the winged beast was quite strong and wasn't easy to defeat.

Warren rushed toward the fiery dragon and struck it with his enchanted diamond sword as Lily threw more snowballs at the flying terror.

"We will defeat this dragon!" Michael called out as he chased the mob boss, clutching his diamond sword.

Simon aimed his arrow at the dragon with its piercing red eyes. The dragon flew close to him and his heart pounded. He took a deep breath and shot the arrow. Simon was shocked and thrilled when the arrow destroyed the beast.

A portal to the End spawned in the center of town. Lily picked up the dragon egg and inspected the portal.

"We can't go to the End," said Michael. "We have to find out what Mr. Anarchy is planning."

Everyone agreed that a trip to the End was pointless, because they had to stop Mr. Anarchy before he staged more attacks.

The townspeople gathered in the center of the village. People were calling out various ideas and opinions. Warren spoke to the crowd. "Quiet!" He raised his voice. "We need to have a meeting."

"Good idea," added Lily. "Let's have a town meeting now. We have to come up with a plan that works for all of us."

The townspeople let out a collective cheer. They were ready to draft a plan that would stop Mr. Anarchy.

As the group waited for the meeting to begin, thunder boomed through the town, and it started to rain.

"His attacks are already starting," Warren called out. "A horde of skeletons is approaching the village—I can see them over there!"

"And zombies, too!" cried Lily.

This was the work of Mr. Anarchy. They had already suffered through many of his attacks, and they knew that he enjoyed summoning storms and mobs to destroy them.

Just then, a lightning bolt shot through the town. It struck a townsperson, and she disappeared.

2
THE MEETING

Lily was too busy battling a gang of skeletons to focus on the missing townsperson. As Lily struck the bony beasts, she hoped another lightning bolt would shoot through the sky and transport her back to the real world. She plunged her diamond sword into the belly of a skeleton, destroying it. While she struck another skeleton, the sun came out, and the hostile mob disappeared.

Warren ran into the center of the town. "We need to have a meeting now."

The town wasn't ready for a meeting. There was chaos in the streets. Townspeople were exhausted after the sudden battle against the Ender Dragon and the hostile mobs. The rain had cleared and they wanted to assess the damage, and they also wanted to discuss what had happened to the missing townsperson. Everyone was talking at the same time and nobody was listening.

Lily couldn't take it. She yelled, "Quiet!"

The crowd stopped talking.

Warren thanked Lily. "Mr. Anarchy has staged another attack. First we had to battle the Ender Dragon and then he summoned a storm. However, this was an extremely powerful storm. During the storm, a lightning bolt struck one of our townspeople, and they were transported back to the Overworld."

"How?" a townsperson with flaming red hair called out.

"We have to find out how she was transported. Once we do, we can all leave this server and return home." Warren almost cried when he said the word home.

Another person called out from the crowd, "I knew the person who was zapped back to the real world. She was my best friend."

"Who was she?" asked Lily.

"Her name was Rebecca. She was a farmer, like me." The townsperson paused. "I'm happy for her. Rebecca wanted to go back home really badly. I'm glad her wish came true."

Lily walked to the townsperson's side to comfort her. "We will all get back home like Rebecca."

"How?" the townsperson wiped the tears from her eyes.

The crowd started to ask, in unison, "How? When?"

Lily announced, "We have to figure out how to summon a powerful storm—one that can produce a lot of lightning that could zap us back to the real world."

"We know," an annoyed townsperson called out. "But how?"

Lily hesitated. She wasn't sure how to summon a powerful storm, but she did have a plan. "We are going to hold a meeting. Everyone must come up with one idea for summoning a storm or getting back to the real world. We will present the ideas, and everyone should be prepared to put their heads together so we can turn those ideas into a plan. If we work together on this, we'll find a way to escape—I'm sure of it!"

The crowd cheered.

However, the cheers turned to cries when the Wither spawned above the village. The powerful, three-headed mob boss was blue, but quickly charged its health bar and turned black. The flying mob created an explosion that destroyed the village library. Then the evil beast unleashed a sea of vile wither skulls, with a trail of smoke rising from the skulls at they exploded. Townspeople attempted to dodge the explosive wither skulls while attacking the floating beast.

Lily ducked as a wither skull shot in her direction. She sighed as she barely missed a blast from the skull. Grabbing her bow and arrow, she aimed at the Wither, striking the center of the beast's body. The Wither lost a heart.

Lily looked in her inventory. She only had a few arrows left, and she was running very low on many resources. "Anyone have arrows I can use?"

Townspeople began to call out. They all had the same response. Everyone was running low on resources.

"How are we going to destroy this beast if we don't have weapons? We are going to have to shoot a lot more arrows to defeat the Wither," Simon worried aloud.

"This battle is way too intense." Michael could barely get the words out. He sprinted toward the Wither with his diamond sword.

"Michael!" Lily called out. She couldn't believe he would get so close to the Wither, and she was worried about her friend. "Be careful."

Lily struck the Wither again. "Good aim," Simon called out.

Warren suggested trying to trap the Wither.

"That's a good idea," Lily told her friends.

Michael struck the beast with his diamond sword, weakening it. Lily dashed over to Michael and said, "Let's lead the Wither to the bedrock prison we built for Mr. Anarchy. It's our only hope. This beast is too powerful to destroy, and we're running out of weapons and potions to fight with."

Michael and Lily clutched their diamond swords. They struck the Wither as the other townspeople shot arrows at the beast. It was growing weaker, but wasn't destroyed.

"We're almost there!" Lily called out.

Suddenly the beast swooped toward Warren, who was standing between two buildings and didn't know where to run. He yelled, "I can't escape!"

As Warren looked frantically for a hiding space, the beast shot a wither skull at him, striking him squarely on the chest and leaving Warren with the Wither effect.

Lily wanted to rush to her friend's side and give him a sip of milk, but she was torn. She had to trap the Wither.

Michael slammed his diamond sword into the Wither again and again, pushing the beast toward the bedrock prison and closing it in.

Everyone cheered, until they heard a sinister laugh boom throughout the town.

3
THE VISIT

"You think you can get back to the real world?" Mr. Anarchy let out a loud, sinister laugh.

"We know we can!" Lily shouted at him.

Mr. Anarchy didn't bother to reply, but instead splashed a potion on Lily, instantly depleting her last heart and destroying her.

"Lily!" Michael cried.

"Do you want to be next?" Mr. Anarchy threatened Michael.

"No," Michael stammered.

Mr. Anarchy let out another shrill laugh, but jumped back when he heard the sound of an explosion.

"It's thunder!" Simon was excited. He hoped this storm would be powerful enough to produce lightning.

Rain fell on the village. Michael got up the courage to race toward Mr. Anarchy, but the sinister villain splashed a potion on himself and disappeared.

"Coward!" Michael called out, but there was no reply.

Lily ran into the center of the town. "Where's Mr. Anarchy?"

Simon replied, "He's gone."

Michael added, "And I don't think he has anything to do with this storm. He appeared shocked when he heard the thunder."

"I hope we see some lightning," Lily exclaimed when they heard more thunder.

"Skeletons!" Michael called out.

"Not again!" Lily wasn't in the mood to battle these bony beasts.

Four skeletons approached the trio and shot arrows at them.

"They got my arm!" Simon called out in pain as he slammed his diamond sword into the skeleton, weakening one of the bony mobs.

Michael splashed potions on the skeletons, destroying one.

Lily searched through her inventory. There was barely anything left. The only way she could battle the skeletons was with her enchanted diamond sword. Lily lunged at the skeletons, striking one and destroying it.

"I don't have any food or potions left," Lily cried to her friends.

Simon struck the final two skeletons, skillfully destroying them.

Warren called out to his friends and sprinted toward them. There was a woman in a blue shirt running next to him.

"Lightning!" Lily called out.

The bolt struck the woman running next to Warren, and she disappeared.

"That was my friend Jane," Warren said as he reached the group and leaned over, hands on his knees, to catch his breath. "I guess she was zapped back to the real world."

As the sun came out and the rain dried, Lily looked at Warren. "It seems like there's a pattern. There's one bolt of lightning and then someone disappears."

Warren looked at the crowd. "There are so many people in the town. If we can only send one person home with each storm, we'll have to live in a perpetual rainstorm. That would be impossible."

"Do you have another idea?" asked Lily.

"No," Warren replied. "But I'll come up with one for before our brainstorming meeting." Warren looked at Lily. He had tears in his eyes.

"Is it your friend?" Lily was worried about Warren.

Her friend nodded. "Yes. Jane was a good friend of mine. I'm happy that she was able to return to the real world, but I'm going to miss her."

"I know it's hard to lose friends. But I just imagine that I'll be able to find them once I get back to my old life," Lily remarked.

"It is hard." Warren sniffled and wiped the tears from his eyes.

Lily thought about her old life often. She wondered what her parents were doing, and if everyone missed her. She also thought about Mrs. Sanders and the kids in their class. It was hard for her to talk about home without crying, so she changed the subject. "Well, we are going to come up with great ideas for our meeting."

"I like your enthusiasm, Lily." Warren smiled.

Michael raced over to them. "I think we have to hold an emergency town meeting right now."

"Why?" Lily questioned.

"Everyone is running low on resources and we need to pool everything we have to survive." Michael paced.

Warren raised his voice and addressed the townspeople as the trio marched into the center of town. A crowd formed around him. As he looked at the faces of his friends and fellow villagers, he announced, "We have an emergency. We are all low on supplies. We must figure out what we need to obtain. I believe we will have to go on mining expeditions."

"Where?" Michael asked.

"We're going to have to travel to a mine. I know there is an abandoned mineshaft in the nearest jungle biome," replied Warren.

Lily suggested, "Michael, Warren, Simon, and I should go on the trip to the mine. We will distribute all of the resources we collect among the townspeople of Lisimi Village."

The townspeople protested. They didn't want to stay behind. A man in a black sweater said, "If we stay here, we might be attacked by Mr. Anarchy, and we don't have any resources to battle him."

A woman with a blue hat said, "We will be too vulnerable if we stay here."

Warren rolled out a different plan. "We should break up into different groups. I have a map that highlights various mines. We will all go on mining trips and meet back to share our resources."

"And remember, we all have to come up with ideas for getting home," Lily added. "We'll still meet when we all return from mining and hunting."

"These trips should inspire us to think of ideas for escaping from this server."

Everyone agreed that this was the best plan. They needed supplies and they also needed to come up with a plan of escape. The townspeople were put in groups, and each set out to a different mine.

Lily and her friends prepared for their trip to the mine. It was getting dark, and they didn't want to arrive at night, when they'd be exposed to hostile mob attacks.

"We should start on our journey," Simon said, looking up at the sky.

"Yes," Warren agreed as he watched the townspeople embark on their mining expeditions.

As the group walked through the village streets, Juan the Butcher raced toward them. "Warren! Lily! Wait!"

"What's the matter?" asked Lily.

Juan was distraught. His voice shook as he said, "Mr. Anarchy has struck again."

4
TRIP TO THE MINE

"**O**h no, what happened here?" Lily exclaimed. She, Warren, and Juan were standing in front of Fred the Farmer's fields. Where once Fred had grown rows and rows of wheat crops, now there was only a blackened hole.

"Someone destroyed most of Fred's wheat with TNT," Juan explained. He sounded distraught.

"This is awful," Lily said. "And I'm sure it's the work of Mr. Anarchy."

"We should be here to tell him when he gets back from helping Emily the Fisherwoman," Juan said. "Mr. Anarchy has been stealing Emily's fish—and now this. Fred will be so upset."

Lily was torn. She wanted to comfort her friend and neighbor, Fred, but she also knew the trip to the mine was vital for their survival. But before she could decide what to do, she heard a voice in the distance. "Warren!"

Fred the Farmer was approaching, and the friends raced to meet their friend before he saw his ruined crops.

"I'm sorry, Fred," said Juan, "but I think you should take a look at your wheat fields."

Fred ran to his farm and cried out when he saw the damage.

"Mr. Anarchy has to be stopped. He can't keep terrorizing us," Lily declared as she followed Fred to comfort him.

"I agree—we can't keep living under threat of attack. But first we have to find some supplies to replenish our inventories," said Michael.

The sky was turning dark. Warren suggested they start on the journey in the morning. The others thought that was a good idea. They walked to their homes.

Lily was happy to have one more night at her small cottage with her pet, Wolfie. She loved the comfort of her home. She said goodbye to her friends and walked toward her small, cozy cottage. As she entered the door, she felt an arrow hit her arm.

"Ouch!" she cried out. Lily realized that she wasn't wearing her armor, leaving her extremely vulnerable to an attack. She tried to retrieve her armor from her inventory, but she didn't have any time. A spider jockey was lunging toward her. The skeleton riding a spider shot a barrage of arrows at an unarmored Lily.

Lily was losing hearts. She cried for help, but her friends couldn't hear her. Lily fumbled for her sword and struck the red-eyed spider with her last bit of strength. The blow weakened the spider, but didn't destroy it.

"Help!" Lily cried out again as another arrow struck her stomach.

Lily had two hearts left when she struck the skeleton with her diamond sword, and was shocked when she destroyed the bony beast. The skeleton dropped a bone, but Lily couldn't pick it up. She was too busy battling the spider. With one last strike, she slayed the spider with her diamond sword. Lily let out a sigh. With the powerful mob defeated, she could take a sip of milk and replenish her hearts.

Lily didn't want to battle any other hostile mobs, so she sprinted into her small cottage. She raced to her bed and jumped beneath the covers. Lily knew that even if she was destroyed, she'd respawn in her own bed, and that made her extremely happy.

In the morning, Michael showed up at Lily's house. "Are you ready for our mining expedition?"

Lily told Michael about the attack from the spider jockey.

"I'm impressed! That's a tough mob. Especially when you're not wearing armor," Michael commended his friend.

They walked outside and met their friends. Warren studied a map. "We don't have to travel very far to reach this mine."

"I hope we find some valuable minerals," Lily said as they walked toward the jungle biome.

"I hope we don't encounter Mr. Anarchy," remarked Simon.

The gang walked along the shoreline. They spotted Emily the Fisherwoman, fishing for her morning catch.

"Hi!" Emily said with a smile.

The group walked over to Emily. "Are you catching a lot?" asked Warren.

"Yes." Emily showed him her pile of fish. "You should take some for your trip. You want to have food to eat. You might be gone a long time. Mining takes a lot of patience."

They thanked her for the fish and continued on their journey to the abandoned mine in the jungle biome. But when they reached the jungle, Warren suddenly looked distraught.

"What's the matter?" asked Lily.

Warren clutched the map, "It doesn't make any sense."

"What?" questioned Simon.

"The abandoned mine was supposed to be here." Warren pointed to a path that was lined with trees. "But I don't see it."

The group explored the area in the jungle, and didn't see the abandoned mineshaft.

"How could that be?" Lily was dumbfounded.

"Do you think we're in the wrong jungle biome?" suggested Michael.

"No." Warren looked at the map again. "I've been here before. I know there is a mine here."

"But it's missing." Simon carefully inspected the ground and the trees. "There are just a bunch of trees."

"I don't like blaming everything on Mr. Anarchy, but I bet he has something to do with the disappearance of the mine." Lily was angry. She wanted to mine and replenish their supplies.

Simon, who had wandered away from the group, still inspecting the area, called out to his friends, "I think I see a hole over here!"

Lily and the others dashed toward Simon. Right on the edge of the jungle biome, there was a hole in the side of a small mountain. Someone had carefully arranged branches and leaves in front of the entrance to the mine to hide it.

"See?" Simon smiled as they all took the scene in. "Someone wanted to make sure it wasn't easy for us to find this place."

"We have to go in!" Michael sprinted inside.

"Wait, it could be a trap!" warned Lily.

The others didn't pay any attention to Lily; they all pulled out their pickaxes and rushed into the abandoned mineshaft.

Kaboom!

5
COMMAND BLOCKS
AND CONTESTS

"**A**re you okay?" Lily called out.

"We're fine!" came Simon's muffled reply.

"It was just a creeper," added Michael. "I think it destroyed someone who was in the mine."

"Who was that?" asked Lily.

"We don't know," replied Simon.

Lily reluctantly walked into the darkened mine. She had a feeling that Mr. Anarchy was going to trap them in the abandoned mineshaft. She was also suspicious of the person who was just destroyed by a silent, explosive attack from a creeper. Lily gripped the pickaxe as if it were a diamond sword. She was ready to attack anyone who entered the mine and startled her.

Michael walked in front of her while the friends talked, testing the blocks around him with his pickaxe.

Finally, he threw up his hands. "This mine seems to be empty!" Michael was annoyed that he still hadn't discovered any minerals.

"You have to give it time. We just have to dig deeper," Simon reassured his friend.

Lily climbed into a hole and banged her pick-axe, hoping to unearth diamonds and other precious minerals.

"Watch out!" Simon warned them. A cave spider crawled by them. Michael hit and destroyed the insect with his diamond sword.

Lily looked up and didn't have enough time to warn Michael that a creeper was behind him.

"Michael!" Simon shouted. But it was too late.

Kaboom!

Michael was destroyed.

Warren shouted, "Look up!"

"That can't be!" Lily cried out.

Two ghasts flew toward them. Simon made a fist and slammed his hand into the fireball the ghast shot at them. The fireball hit the ghast, and it exploded.

Lily used her fist to destroy the second ghast.

"I knew Mr. Anarchy was plotting something," Lily called out, looking around for other mobs. She was discouraged, but she was happy when Simon yelled.

"Diamonds!" Simon exclaimed. "I found diamonds."

They gang gathered the blue diamonds and filled their inventories with the precious stones.

"Lily! Simon! Warren!" Michael called to his friends.

"We're in the mine. We found diamonds!" Lily was losing count of the precious gems as she collected them.

"Lisimi Village is in trouble." Michael frowned. "I TPed back here to warn you guys. There were zombie pigmen walking through the town in the middle of the day. Someone is spawning Nether mobs in the Overworld."

"We know! We just fought a ghast," explained Simon.

"Oh no!" Lily looked up and spotted four blazes fly through the dimly-lit mine. The fiery, flying beasts shot fireballs at the group.

"Does anybody have a snowball?" asked Lily as she grabbed her sword. She was out of arrows.

"No, I have nothing," Michael replied. Everyone else checked their inventories, but they were all close to empty.

Lily attempted to shield herself from the blazes' powerful blasts, but she was struck by a fireball and destroyed.

Moments later, Lily respawned in her bed in the cottage. She hurried outside to see if her friends had also been destroyed.

"Simon!" Lily called to her neighbor.

Simon ran out of his house. "Lily, are you okay?"

"I'm fine," Lily said. "You, too?"

"Yes. Are the diamonds still in your inventory, or did you lose them when you were in the mine?" Simon asked.

Lily was relieved when she found her diamonds safely in her inventory. "They're here."

"This is a crazy invasion of Nether mobs," Simon said as two zombie pigmen walked by them.

"Why is Mr. Anarchy doing this to us?" Lily was very upset.

Michael and Warren emerged from their houses. They had also been destroyed in the mine by the Nether mobs.

"We're going to have to go to the Nether to fight these mobs. We have to brew potions of fire resistance," said Warren.

"We should also travel to the cold biome to gather snowballs," suggested Lily. "If we have a large supply of those, we'll be able to defeat the Nether mobs."

Michael pointed out, "We have to defeat Mr. Anarchy. Once we do that, the Nether mobs will disappear."

"But we also have to survive," Lily replied. "And the mobs won't just go away on their own, even if we can stop Mr. Anarchy from spawning more."

Townspeople returned from their mining trips and walked up to the group.

Everyone in the town told stories about encountering Nether mobs in the Overworld.

"We saw blazes, ghasts and magma cubes," an exhausted townsperson informed them.

Warren said, "We know there are Nether mobs spawning in the Overworld. We have to battle them.

We think Mr. Anarchy is the one summoning these Nether mobs."

Lily added, "We have to destroy Mr. Anarchy."

A townsperson called out, "No, we don't. We just have to make our way home. Are we finally having that meeting where we each present our ideas for getting back to the real world?"

Warren agreed and announced, "Town meeting. Who has an idea they'd like to share?"

Lily asked if she could be the first person to present.

"Okay," Warren said, and he introduced Lily to the crowd.

Lily disliked speaking in front of lots of people. Her heart raced as she explained her plan to the townsfolk.

"As far as we can tell, the only people who have been sent home have been struck by a lightning bolt. So if we can create lightning and make sure it strikes each of us, we should be able to get home. We could use command blocks to create lightning—although we'll need to be able to replicate the lightning bolt many times, because we have to create one for each player in order to get all of us back home," Lily said.

Everyone was enthusiastic about Lily's plan. There was just one problem.

"The only problem is that I'm out of command blocks," Lily said.

The crowd erupted in cries of dismay.

"Does anyone have command blocks?" Lily called over the crowd's noise.

A murmuring went through the crowd as towns-people checked their inventories for command blocks and talked among themselves.

But when the gathering fell silent, Lily was devastated. No one had any of the rare blocks.

Slowly, the townsperson in the blue hat raised her hand. "I was just in the jungle biome, where Mr. Anarchy has his temple. I noticed he had a redstone comparator that could only be powered by a command block. He must have a store of them somewhere."

Warren beckoned the woman up onto the stage. "What's your name?" he asked. "And can you tell us more?"

"I'm Harriet," the woman in the blue hat told them. "I also spotted a person in a green jumpsuit by Mr. Anarchy's jungle temple."

"Great observations," Warren commended Harriet. "Thanks for letting us know about this." Warren then asked if anyone else had a plan for getting back to the real world.

There wasn't time for a reply. The sky grew dark and rain fell on the crowd. In moments, the town was overrun with zombies and skeletons.

Arrows shot through the air. The town fought hard to destroy these hostile mobs. Yet despite having an inventory overflowing with diamonds, Lily didn't have any arrows. She fought skeletons and zombies with her diamond sword instead.

A lightning bolt flashed through the rainy skies.

"Harriet!" Warren called out as the bolt of lightning struck Harriet. But it was too late—she had already disappeared.

Four blazes flew through the sky, and Warren and the others couldn't focus on Harriet's disappearance. They were too busy trying to survive the storm.

Fireballs rained down on them along with the rain. Lily sprinted away from a fireball, but it struck Michael and he was destroyed. Lily turned around to see that Michael was gone. She held her sword and slammed it into a skeleton, destroying it. She paused to wipe the rain from her face.

A few townspeople had snowballs in their inventories, and they aimed at the flying Nether mobs, destroying them.

The rain stopped, and Michael dashed out of his house and into the center of the village.

Juan the Butcher stood in front of the blacksmith's shop. He advised everyone, "Trade your diamonds and other resources for swords and armor. We have a serious battle ahead of us."

Warren ran over to Lily. "Can you believe Harriet was transported back to the real world?"

"She was going to lead us to Mr. Anarchy's command blocks." Lily was upset. She wanted to get command blocks from Mr. Anarchy and summon a storm with endless lightning bolts so the entire population of Lisimi Village could return to the real world. "Now what will we do?"

6
BATTLE IN THE JUNGLE

"We have to search Mr. Anarchy's jungle temple for his command blocks right away," demanded Michael.

"I want to start looking now, too," said Warren, "but we need to have a plan."

As they spoke, six magma cubes bounced toward them. Lily sprinted toward the magma cubes, cutting one of the cubes in half. The smaller cubes jumped at Lily. She tried to slay them with her diamond sword, but the cubes surrounded her, and Lily lost a heart.

"Help!" she cried out.

Michael destroyed two small cubes with his diamond sword. The others joined and defeated the bouncy cubes from the Nether.

"We have to see Mr. Anarchy now. I want this Nether invasion to stop." Lily was exhausted from battle.

The group ran through the grassy biome toward the jungle, but halfway there, Lily let out a muffled cry and disappeared.

"Lily?" Michael turned around and didn't see his friend.

"I'm down here," Lily called out. She had fallen into a hole in the ground and landed in a minecart. "Where do you think this goes?"

"Only one way to find out," Warren said with a shrug. He looked at the others, and they all nodded.

The gang hopped into minecarts and traveled straight underground for a long while. When they came to a stop and climbed out of the carts, they were in another hole right under the entrance to Mr. Anarchy's jungle temple.

But as they emerged from the mineshaft, arrows flew at them.

"Shield yourself," Lily called out.

"There's no way you can protect yourself from my powerful army," Mr. Anarchy said with a smile. "Why did you even bother coming here? You knew I would just destroy you."

Lily didn't listen to Mr. Anarchy. She leapt at the evil griefer and struck him with her enchanted diamond sword.

Mr. Anarchy laughed and shrugged off the attack. "Haven't we gone through this before? You're not going to win."

"But—" Lily said, but before she could finish her sentence, Mr. Anarchy splashed a potion on her and she was destroyed.

Lily woke up in her bed in the cottage. She could hear Wolfie barking. "Wolfie," Lily said to her tame wolf, "I feel like we're never going to beat Mr. Anarchy. Why is he so mean? I just want to go home."

With a sigh, Lily stepped out of her house. She was about to head to the minecarts that lead to the jungle when she thought better of it. Instead, she loped into town and tracked down Ilana the Alchemist. Ilana always had an array of potions. Since the town had gone treasure hunting to restore their resources, Lily knew Ilana would have a bunch of potions on hand. Lily took out a couple of diamonds from her inventory.

"Ilana, I'd like a potion of invisibility." Lily handed Ilana the diamonds.

"For two diamonds, you can get a few more potions," Ilana said, showing Lily her trunk, which was filled to the brim with bottles.

"I think I'd like some potions that harm and weaken. I have to defeat Mr. Anarchy." Lily grabbed the potions and rushed to the jungle biome.

When Lily finally arrived, her friends were immersed in a serious battle. Mr. Anarchy had increased his army since the last battle, and blue soldiers outnumbered her allies.

She wanted to help her friends, but with everyone distracted by the battle, Lily realized that this was her opportunity to search for the command blocks and summon a storm. Lily splashed a potion of invisibility herself and crept into the jungle temple to explore.

The jungle temple was massive, and she searched room after room for the command blocks. Lily picked her way through a room cluttered with blocks of all kinds, looking for the distinctive green and grey of command blocks. But when she glimpsed a bit of green between two other blocks, Lily got careless. She tripped over a block and made a sound, and Mr. Anarchy appeared.

"Hello?" he called out. "I know someone is there."

Lily remained quiet. She spotted the command blocks and snuck toward them, trying not to make a sound.

"You can't hide from me," Mr. Anarchy threatened.

Lily wanted to place the command blocks in her inventory, but if Mr. Anarchy saw the blocks move, he would know where she was.

"It's just a matter of time before you reappear, Lily," Mr. Anarchy taunted.

Lily's heart skipped a beat. She couldn't understand how Mr. Anarchy knew it was her standing by the command blocks.

Then she looked down, and she almost cried out. She could see her hand, floating on its own in the room. Lily's potion was losing its potency. A moment later, Lily was visible.

Mr. Anarchy pointed his sword at Lily. She grabbed her sword from her inventory, ready to battle the griefer, when cries were heard in the distance. "Help!" It sounded as though, somehow, Lily's friends had overwhelmed Mr. Anarchy's army.

Mr. Anarchy ran outside, leaving Lily alone with his huge supply command blocks.

Lily couldn't believe her luck. She looked around quickly, trying to count the number of blocks and wondering if they would be enough to send the whole town home.

Just as she was reaching for the first command block to place in her inventory, a whistling sound filled her ears, and an arrow struck her in the back. She cried out and moved to shield herself, but Mr. Anarchy's guards had arrived and she was quickly overwhelmed. As arrows landed from all sides, Lily was destroyed.

She respawned a moment later in her bungalow, and though she'd been destroyed, she felt determined. She was nowhere close to giving up. She knew where Mr. Anarchy kept his command blocks, and she was going to retrieve them.

Lily traveled back to the jungle temple. It was almost dark when she arrived. She emerged from the mineshaft in front of the temple and dashed inside. But she didn't go unnoticed—as she ran into the building, an arrow pierced her arm.

Lily kept running. As she traversed the halls, she didn't see her friends or the blue soldiers. In fact, it was eerily calm, and this made her nervous. As she walked further into the temple and reached the room full of command blocks, she heard a voice. If someone stepped into the hallway now, there'd be no place for her to hide. She had to get to cover, so she kept running until she reached the room she'd been caught in earlier. As she crossed the threshold, an arrow struck her leg.

"You're not going anywhere," said Mr. Anarchy.

Lily stood frozen in terror, her leg throbbing. Mr. Anarchy and his army were pointing their bows and arrows at her.

"Your friends are in prison. And that's where you're going, too," Mr. Anarchy announced.

Lily put her head down. She remembered the jungle temple's prison cells all too well from her last visit here, when she and her friends had been held for days.

Mr. Anarchy escorted her to the prison cell. Though Lily was sad about being trapped, she was also relieved that she'd see her friends again. But when Mr. Anarchy opened the door, she was shocked to see the prison was empty.

7
MR. ANARCHY STRIKES AGAIN

Lily's heart was pounding. She was alone in the prison cell. "Michael! Warren! Simon!"

She heard only silence.

"Someone? Can anybody hear me?" Lily looked up at the ceiling. She recalled the last time she was trapped in this prison cell. Mr. Anarchy had created a hole in the ceiling, where he'd watch his prisoners battle hostile mobs. To Lily's surprise, there wasn't any light emanating from the ceiling now. Maybe he didn't watch his inmates battle anymore. With that concern out of the way, Lily had to plot her escape.

She searched through her inventory. She didn't have enough obsidian to craft a portal to the Nether. She had a pickaxe, but she imagined knocking down the wall would draw attention to her, and then Mr. Anarchy would probably pay a visit. Lily was feeling helpless. She stood in the prison and ate an apple to regain her strength.

The prison door opened and Mr. Anarchy called out, "You have a roommate."

A woman wearing a black sweater and pants walked into the room. She stared at Lily.

"Who are you?" asked the woman in black.

"I'm Lily," she replied quietly. "And you are?"

"I'm Robin." She looked shaken.

"It's okay," Lily comforted Robin.

"I don't know what happened," Robin remarked. "Am I actually in the Overworld? It can't be."

"Yes," Lily sighed. "This is the Overworld."

"But I was just playing at my house and I was zapped into the game," Robin cried.

"Was there a storm when you were playing?" asked Lily.

"Yes," Robin was shocked Lily knew there had been a storm outside when she was playing Minecraft on her mom's laptop.

"We're all trapped in here," Lily informed her. "But I know a way to get out of this server."

"How?" The woman was eager to hear how she could escape from the Overworld.

"We have to summon a lightning bolt, but we need command blocks," explained Lily.

"Do you have command blocks?" asked Robin.

"No, but Mr. Anarchy does, and we can get them from him." Lily paced in the small room. A cave spider crawled on the floor, and she grabbed her diamond sword from her inventory and slammed it against the insect.

"But we're trapped in here," Robin reminded Lily. "I tried to survive in the Overworld, but he caught me within a few minutes. It's very hard to live here in real life. It's not like the game at all. I had a skeleton attack me. As I watched the arrow fly toward me, I realized this was a lot more hardcore than playing at home."

While Robin spoke, the door opened. Mr. Anarchy smiled. "Did somebody say 'hardcore'?"

Robin paused. "No," she stammered. "I wasn't talking about Hardcore mode, if that's what you mean."

"And Lily, you'll never get my command blocks. And I just might use those command blocks to put you on Hardcore mode." He closed the door.

Lily wanted to ask him where her friends were trapped, but she didn't have time. She looked at Robin. "Don't worry. He's threatened to put us on Hardcore mode before. I think it's just a threat."

"How do you know?" Robin's voice quivered.

"I just do." Lily thought for a minute about why she felt so sure that Mr. Anarchy's threats were hollow. "I think if Mr. Anarchy were going to destroy us, he'd have done it by now. For some reason, he wants to keep us around."

Robin stood by the wall. "Do you hear something?"

Lily paused. She walked over to Robin. There was a muffled voice coming from the other side of the wall. "I think there's someone back there," she said.

Robin grabbed her pickaxe and banged it against the wall. A few pieces of the wall crumbled to the ground. She called out, "Do you hear us?"

There was no reply. Robin and Lily turned around when Mr. Anarchy opened the door and yelled, "There is no escaping. How many times do I have to warn you?" He was infuriated. "I am going to punish you!"

Mr. Anarchy slammed the door shut. Two skeletons spawned in front of the girls.

"Help!" Robin called out in terror.

Lily leapt at the bony skeleton, diminishing its health bar with her diamond sword. Robin stood next to Lily and didn't fight.

"You have to help me, Robin!" Lily called to her new friend. "You can't let the skeletons destroy you."

Robin fumbled with her diamond sword, striking the weakened skeleton and destroying him with a single blow.

"Good job!" Lily exclaimed as she splashed a potion on the other skeleton and destroyed it.

"How are we going to get out of here?" Robin looked at Lily, distressed.

Lily remembered how she and Simon had last escaped this cell, and she asked Robin, "Do you have any obsidian?"

8
NETHER AGAIN

As the two quickly crafted a portal to the Nether, Lily could hear the voice coming from the other side of the wall. It was growing louder, and Lily could recognize who it belonged to: It was Michael. She wanted to help her friend, but she was surrounded by purple mist. Within seconds, Lily was no longer in the cell, but rather in the fiery Nether biome.

Two blazes shot past them. "Maybe they didn't see us?" Robin said hopefully.

"I hope so. Being in the Nether is very challenging for me. It's not like playing at home. This is the one place that I will never fully master," Lily confessed to Robin.

The two trekked through the red Nether landscape, avoiding falling into a stream of lava while dodging blasts from the blazes.

"I knew they'd be back," Lily said as she grabbed her arrow and aimed at the yellow mob with black eyes.

"Bulls-eye!" Robin called out when her arrow struck the flying mob.

"Wow, you're a skilled fighter," Lily remarked as she tried to destroy the blaze.

"I was a known fighter in the Overworld. In fact, I was invited to this server to be in a battle," explained Robin.

"Someone invited you to join this server? Who?" Lily asked.

"I don't know them very well. Their screen name is Leon." Robin replied, and then pointed out four ghasts that were flying toward them.

"I've never heard of Leon." Lily wondered who this player was and if he lived in Lisimi Village. She wanted to know who would be evil enough to recruit people on this server that trapped you in the Overworld.

The ghasts approached the girls. They made chirping sounds as the flying white mob shot powerful fireballs at them.

Lily used her fist to hit the powerful ball, and it destroyed the ghast. "One down."

Robin was able to seamlessly destroy two ghasts with her fists.

"You make it look so easy." Lily was impressed.

Robin annihilated the final ghast. "We should go back to the Overworld," suggested Robin.

"I agree, but I think we should try to gather some supplies while we're down here. Our entire village has been on mining trips to replenish our supplies. Nobody has traveled to the Nether, and we need to get Nether wart to brew potions."

"But that means we have to find a Nether fortress," Robin exclaimed. "That's almost impossible to find!"

"I know, but we're going to have to try," said Lily.

"I don't think that's a good idea." Robin wanted to leave the Nether.

Lily wondered if Robin was right. Her thoughts were preoccupied with Michael. She knew he was trapped in the Mr. Anarchy's prison, and she wanted to help him escape. She said, "You're right, Robin. Let's get back to the Overworld. We have to help my friend, Michael, escape from Mr. Anarchy's jungle prison, and we also have to get our hands on those command blocks."

The girls were about to hop on a portal back to the Overworld when they heard a familiar voice in the distance.

"Michael?" Lily said, and she ran toward the voice. Robin followed closely behind.

They could see someone behind a pillar, but when they reached the pillar, the person disappeared.

"Where did they go?" asked Lily.

"Do you think we're being tricked?" Robin was suspicious of everything since she arrived on this new server.

The voice called out again, "Help! Over here!"

Lily looked up. "Where are you?"

Robin stared ahead. "Do you see that? It looks like a Nether fortress!"

The two sprinted toward the fortress. "Do you think he's in here?" asked Lily.

"Help!" The voice grew louder.

"I think so," replied Robin as she destroyed the blaze that guarded the Nether fortress.

Michael's voice wailed, "I'm in here! There are magma cubes!"

A half-dozen large magma cubes surrounded Michael. Lily and Robin struck the cubes, but they broke into smaller cubes. The trio was battling numerous cubes, and they were losing hearts quickly. Lily wanted to grab milk from her inventory, but she didn't have time.

Robin skillfully destroyed two magma cubes and the smaller cubes.

Michael obliterated the final cubes, and Lily offered all of them milk.

"How did you get to the Nether?" asked Lily as she took a sip.

"I was trapped in the cell with a person named Leon. He acted like he was my friend, but once we got down here, he tried to destroy me. I think he's working with Mr. Anarchy," said Michael.

"Leon!" Robin shook with fury. "That's the name of the player who invited me to join this server and got me trapped here."

"We have to watch out. He might be here. I was able to win the battle and destroy him, but I think he might be looking for me here."

"I wonder if that's who we saw appearing and disappearing when we heard you calling for help," Robin said.

Michael walked through the fortress, inspecting each room for Leon.

"Where are the others?" Lily asked as she picked Nether wart that grew near the staircase.

"Simon and Warren were able to escape. I thought you were with them. I assume they are back at Lisimi Village."

"I was the only who was destroyed. I respawned there, and they weren't in the village," said Lily.

Michael gasped. "Then we have to find them!"

"And we have to destroy Leon." Robin wanted revenge on the person who trapped her on the server.

"Did I hear someone say my name?" A man dressed in orange appeared in the entrance of the Nether fortress. He splashed a potion of weakness on the trio.

"Leon!" Michael was weakened by the potion, and used what little strength he had to lunge at the orange griefer.

Leon shielded himself from Michael's sword and splashed another potion on Michael. He grabbed his sword and destroyed Michael with one strike.

"Michael!" Lily cried.

Leon looked at Lily. "You're next."

9
RESCUE MISSION

"**N**ever!" Lily reached into her inventory and splashed a potion of invisibility on Robin and herself.

Robin was invisible. She didn't know where Lily was, but she used the opportunity to escape from Leon. She sprinted out of the fortress into the Nether landscape. Two zombie pigmen walked by her as she began to reappear. She looked for Lily, but no matter how many times she called her name, she didn't get a response. Robin was beginning to lose hope, when she heard Lily call out, "Robin!"

"Where are you, Lily?" Robin couldn't find her friend.

"I'm over here." Lily ran to Robin's side and pointed out, "There are three ghasts flying in our direction. We have to get out of here before they attack us."

"Or before Leon returns," said Robin as she quickly constructed a portal and they hopped on. The purple mist surrounded the duo, and they emerged in the center of Lisimi Village.

"There's a big roller coaster over here, right?" Robin looked at the familiar landscape.

"Yes. We are the ones who built it. Once we win this battle, we can ride the roller coaster," Lily said.

Lily hoped that there would be peace and they could ride the roller coaster one more time before they returned to the real world. The only highlight of being trapped on the server was being able to ride the crazy-fast coaster in real time.

Lily was jolted back to reality when she spotted seven ghasts shooting through the sky. The white, blocky mobs opened their red eyes and unleashed a series of chirping sounds as they shot lethal fireballs at a group of helpless townspeople, instantly destroying them.

"We need to help!" Lily sprinted toward the ghasts and used her arrow to destroy two of them.

Robin annihilated the remaining ghasts as Juan the Butcher ran toward them. "Those villagers who were just destroyed were my friends. We have to check on them," he said.

Lily nodded. "Can you show us where they live?"

Juan waved his hand for them to follow, then ran to a cluster of houses on the outskirts of town. Lily knocked on the door of the first, but no one answered. The house was silent.

Juan was already running to the next house, hesitating only a moment after knocking before opening the door. "There's no one here," he said, walking back out of the empty house.

"But where could they have gone?" Robin asked. "Are you sure they came back from their mining trips in time to sleep in their homes last night?"

Juan nodded. "Yes, I saw them come home."

"Then what happened to them after they were destroyed?" Robin asked.

Lily's lips were tightly pursed. "It looks like they didn't respawn."

Robin gasped. "But how can that be?"

Juan and Lily shared a glance. "It could be that Mr. Anarchy put them on Hardcore mode," Lily said. "But I really thought he wanted to keep us alive. Maybe there's something special about these mobs?"

"There were regular skeleton and zombies in the village last night, and everyone that they destroyed respawned just fine," Juan said.

"Juan, you have to believe we'll do everything we can to find out what happened to your friends." Lily put a hand on Juan's shoulder. "Now, have you seen Warren and Simon?"

"No," said Juan. "I thought they were with you. But I did see Michael."

Lily hoped Mr. Anarchy hadn't used his command blocks to put everyone on Hardcore mode. Maybe she was wrong about his threat of putting them on Hardcore mode being empty.

"What are we going to do?" asked Robin.

Lily didn't know, but she was relieved when she heard Michael's voice call out to her. "Lily! I have good news."

Lily was excited to hear something nice for a change. She didn't want to tell him about the Nether attack and how many townspeople were destroyed and hadn't respawned in their beds.

"Simon and Warren are trapped in Mr. Anarchy's prison. And so is Leon," Michael told Lily.

Lily sighed. "What about that is good news?"

"At least we know where they are and we can rescue them," Michael rationalized.

Lily properly introduced Robin to Michael, and the trio sprinted toward the minecarts, ready to save their friends from Mr. Anarchy's prison. On the way there, Lily explained what happened to the townspeople.

Michael frowned. "I seriously hope Mr. Anarchy didn't put them on Hardcore mode."

They all agreed that they had to find out what had happened to the townspeople, but first they had to rescue their friends, Simon and Warren.

As they approached the jungle temple, Lily suggested they splash a potion of invisibility on themselves so they could sneak in. The trio did just that and walked into the temple, following the sound of Michael's soft footsteps to the room where their friends were being held.

"They are trapped in this room," Michael said in a hushed voice.

"What's Mr. Anarchy playing at? He put them right next to his hidden stash of command blocks," said Lily.

"Should we try and take a few?" Robin asked.

The trio agreed and started picked up command blocks. Lily wondered why Mr. Anarchy didn't have a blue griefer guarding the command blocks or the prison cell. She was suspicious and worried they were about to be trapped. She couldn't bear spending another minute in one of Mr. Anarchy's small, dirty, mob-ridden prison cells.

As they put the last of the blocks in their inventories, Michael said, "We are beginning to reappear. Do you have any more potion?"

Lily checked, but her inventory was empty. She shook her head.

Robin had a bottle of potion, but it was barely enough for one of them. "I'm sorry. I don't even have enough for me."

"We're going to have to break down this door." Michael stood in front of the door to the small prison cell.

The group had to rescue their friends quickly, before Mr. Anarchy and the blue griefers attacked them.

"Look who came to visit me." A loud voice rose through the jungle temple. "Did you bring me any presents?" He laughed.

"We've come to save our friends," Lily shouted at the sinister griefer.

"You think I'm just going to let them go?"

Michael leapt at Mr. Anarchy with his sword, but two blue griefers stopped him. They struck Michael with their diamond swords.

Mr. Anarchy called to his soldiers, "Leave him alone. I don't want to destroy him. I want to imprison him."

Lily didn't want to be trapped in a cell, but she was afraid of being destroyed. She feared she wouldn't respawn, like the townspeople hadn't returned after being destroyed in the attack of the Nether mobs. But as she followed Mr. Anarchy to a cell, Michael, Lily, and Robin trailing behind her, something dawned on Lily: Mr. Anarchy had said he didn't want Michael destroyed. So she *was* right! Mr. Anarchy wanted to keep them alive . . . but why?

Mr. Anarchy and the blue griefers led Michael, Lily, and Robin to a cell. Mr. Anarchy said, "Welcome to your new home."

Mr. Anarchy opened the door to the small prison cell. Lily was happy to see Warren and Simon, but her smile turned to a scowl when she saw Leon standing next to them.

10
PRISONERS

"**L**ily!" Simon was happy to see his friend.

Lily couldn't pay attention to Simon and Warren, because she was fixated on Leon.

"Who are you, and what do you want from us?" Lily took out her diamond sword and pointed it at Leon.

"What's wrong with Leon?" asked Simon. "He's nice."

"No, he isn't." Michael also took out his diamond sword and brushed it against Leon's face. "He trapped me in the Nether. He isn't a good person."

Robin added, "He invited me onto this server so he could trap me here."

"You're a griefer?" Warren was shocked.

"No!" Leon fumbled with his words. "I'm not. I'm—"

"There are no excuses that can save you. You've destroyed my life. I'm trapped on this server and all I want to do is go home." Robin held a potion of harming next to Leon and threatened to splash it on him.

"I can explain!" Leon shouted.

"Okay, tell us." Lily moved closer and her diamond sword touched Leon's chest.

Leon tried to move away from the diamond swords, but Lily and Michael stood next to him. He spoke. "I'm sorry, Robin. Mr. Anarchy promised to help me get off the server and go home, if I found a replacement for him. That's how I found you. I just wanted you to come here and work for Mr. Anarchy."

"I'd never do that!" Robin shouted, hoping Mr. Anarchy could hear how much she disliked him.

"Well, I was desperate. I wanted to go home. So, I found you on a server and I led you into this world. And I'm so sorry about that, I really am."

Robin didn't know if she should accept his apology. She said, "You'd better help me get back home."

"I will. I promise," he looked at Robin. "Just put the potion away."

Robin put the potion back in her inventory. "You'd better start thinking of ways to get me back home. Obviously you can't even find your own way home, so I'm not sure how you can help me."

Michael wanted to know why Leon had tried to destroy him when he was in the Nether. "I thought we were friends, but once we got into the Nether, you attacked me. Why?"

"It was Mr. Anarchy's idea. He wanted me to find Lily and Robin. I knew if you figured out that I was chasing your friends, you wouldn't help me. But I knew that if they heard you call for help, they'd come to your rescue—and walk right into my trap."

Warren asked, "Are you still working for Mr. Anarchy?"

"Yes," Leon replied softly, "but I don't want to help an evil griefer. I just want to go home. If you guys can get me back to the real world, then I will help you defeat Mr. Anarchy."

Lily wondered if Leon was telling the truth. She also wondered if Leon knew any secrets that could help them defeat the evil Mr. Anarchy.

Lily questioned him, "How can you help us defeat Mr. Anarchy?"

Leon replied. "I'm not sure. But I do have some command blocks in my inventory, which can help us a lot. I know Mr. Anarchy turned off the cheats for this server, and the command blocks would be very helpful."

Lily looked at Robin. She didn't want Leon to know that she had command blocks. She wasn't just going to trust Leon, because he had to earn her trust. Lily was happy that Robin didn't reveal that she had command blocks, either.

"Do you know any of Mr. Anarchy's secrets?" asked Michael.

Leon smiled. "I know one."

"What is it?" Michael demanded.

"He really wants to go back to the real world. He has a team working around the clock trying to get back to the real world. We are all experiments to him. He only attacks players on the server so he can figure out how to get back home." Leon blurted this information.

Lily gasped. "That explains why he'll torture us, but he won't destroy us! Could he be thinking of experimenting on us?"

"I don't know, but maybe he wants to keep the option open." Leon sighed. "That's the team I wanted to join. I was hoping I'd be able to leave if I could be a part of one of his experiments. He's zapped a bunch of people back. The problem is that it doesn't work every time. At first he believed he could get home simply by summoning a lightning bolt, but it's a lot more complicated than that," he explained.

"Where does the team work?" asked Robin.

"He has a room right down the hall. He recruited many skilled players to help him get out. We chose you, Robin, because you're a skilled fighter. We wanted to amass a team of top-rated players, because we felt they knew the game."

Robin was happy to hear that she was chosen for her skills, but she was still angry that they had trapped her on this server.

Robin asked, "What other ways has Mr. Anarchy tried to escape?"

Leon didn't have a chance to finish telling them about Mr. Anarchy's attempts at escaping from the Overworld, because two skeletons spawned in the small room.

"We have to defeat these mobs," Lily cried. "There was an attack in Lisimi Village, and the townspeople never respawned. We still don't know why."

"Do you think they respawned in the real world?" Simon asked, ducking to avoid a fireball.

The bony mobs shot dozens of arrows at the group. Robin leaped out of the way of an arrow, but the prison cell was very small, and there was no place to hide.

Lily thrust her diamond sword at a skeleton, striking the vicious mob in the belly.

"You got it!" Michael called out as the beast was destroyed.

"We still have one more left," Lily aimed at the other skeleton.

Leon cried out as the skeleton shuffled toward him.

"Strike it with your sword!" exclaimed Lily.

Leon reached for his diamond sword, but it was too late. The skeleton hit Leon with a barrage of arrows, destroying him.

Lily's arrow struck the beast and destroyed the last skeleton.

"Where's Leon?" asked Michael.

"He's gone." Lily paused. "And he might not respawn."

"Maybe he made his way back to the real world." Michael hoped this was true. Although they had had issues with Leon, they wanted everyone to escape safely from the server.

"Or maybe he was destroyed in both worlds." Lily shook as these words fell from her mouth.

The door opened, Mr. Anarchy entered and asked, "Did you enjoy battling the ghasts?"

"Where's Leon?" Lily demanded.

Mr. Anarchy smiled. "You'll never know."

11
SOMETHING SINISTER

Lily grabbed a potion of harming from her inventory and doused Mr. Anarchy.

"Attack him!" she called out to the others.

Michael and Simon stormed over to Mr. Anarchy, striking the sinister villain with their diamond swords.

"Stop!" Mr. Anarchy cried. "I'll let you know about Leon."

They didn't listen to Mr. Anarchy. They struck him with their swords, just as two skeletons spawned in the small prison cell.

"Oh no!" Mr. Anarchy called out.

A skeleton shot an arrow at Mr. Anarchy. He was destroyed by his own creation.

"We have to get out of here!" Lily called to her friends.

The group darted from the prison. They scurried down the hall of the jungle temple, dodging arrows from the blue griefers that monitored the hall.

"Faster!" Lily cried to the group.

They ran as fast as they could, until they exited the jungle temple. Lily hid behind a large patch of leaves. The others joined her. They grabbed their bows and arrows from their inventories and shot arrows at the blue griefers.

Michael spotted someone rushing past the soldiers. "Do you see that person?"

"Yes." Lily paused, taking a second look at the person. "It looks like Leon."

"So he respawned!" Michael exclaimed.

"That's true. I don't know where or why," Lily said as she shot an arrow at a blue griefer. "But we are going to find out."

Robin said, "We should get out of here."

"Not so fast." Michael hit another blue griefer and destroyed him. "I think we should stick around and see where Leon is hiding. I don't trust him. And I have a feeling he is planning something with Mr. Anarchy."

"But our town is under attack," Lily reminded him.

"I know, but we'd be better off helping them out if we stay here. We want to destroy Mr. Anarchy, and this is the place to do it," Michael said.

The gang destroyed four blue griefers, but they respawned in the jungle temple. Lily said, "This is pointless. We keep destroying them and they just emerge from Mr. Anarchy's house. We have to come up with another plan."

The sky turned dark and rain started to fall on the group. The griefers looked as surprised by the rainstorm as Lily and her friends. "I don't think Mr. Anarchy planned this," Lily noted.

Skeletons and zombies spawned in the jungle temple, as magma cubes bounced toward the blue griefers. The gang hid behind the bark of a large tree and watched the blue griefers struggle to defeat the undead mobs and the cubes from the Nether.

"This is our chance to escape," Robin exclaimed.

The group reluctantly headed back to the town. Although they wanted to defeat Mr. Anarchy and find out about Leon, they knew a rainstorm could destroy them all.

The gang found the hole in the ground where they kept the minecarts and each hopped into their own cart. When they arrived at Lisimi Village, Emily the Fisherwoman greeted them.

"We've had another attack from the Nether mobs, and we've lost more townspeople," Emily said.

Fred the Farmer walked over to Emily's side. "And people have spotted the person in a green jumpsuit roaming around town."

Emily added, "I heard the person in the green jumpsuit has blocks of TNT."

Michael asked, "Has anything been blown up?"

"Not yet," Emily replied.

The remaining townspeople gathered around the group. Lily looked at the dwindling crowd. She couldn't believe the town had become so small. She hoped the people who were destroyed were zapped back to the real world, and she wished one of them would contact them.

Lily asked, "Has anybody heard from a townsperson that disappeared?"

Nobody had.

"Why would anyone reenter this server? They would be stuck in the Overworld," replied a townsperson.

Lily knew this was true. She just wished she knew what happened once someone was destroyed by a Nether mob or an End mob. Lily realized that when she destroyed a blue griefer with her arrow, the blue griefer had respawned. And Leon had respawned after being destroyed by a skeleton. She wondered if the Nether and End mobs were more powerful, or if Mr. Anarchy had put certain players on Hardcore mode with command blocks, while he let others stay on Survival mode.

Night was beginning to fall in Lisimi Village. Warren announced, "Everyone should go home for the night. We don't want to leave ourselves vulnerable to hostile mob attacks. In the morning, we will have another town meeting."

The townspeople agreed and left the center of the town.

"I don't have a place to stay," Robin told her new friends.

"You can stay with me," Lily said. "I have an extra bedroom in my cottage."

Robin thanked Lily.

Lily was exhausted and excited to spend the night in her small cottage with Wolfie.

"I hope you don't mind playing with Wolfie. He's my pet wolf," Lily told Robin as they walked toward the cottage.

"I love pets. Back in the real world, I have a pet cat named Pepper and a dog named Peanut." Robin had tears in her eyes when she talked about her pets. She wanted to return home.

"I have pets in the real world, too." Lily didn't want to talk about her pets. She missed them too much. Instead, Lily focused on her cottage. She felt very comfortable there, and it was the closest thing she had to a home now. Lily pointed at the cottage in the distance. "We're almost there."

As she approached the cottage, Lily heard a loud explosion.

Kaboom!

"My house!" Lily cried.

Someone had blown up Lily's cottage.

12
SKELETON SCUFFLE

Warren rushed over to Lily. "What happened?" "Somebody destroyed my house," Lily cried. The sky was growing dark. Warren suggested, "You guys can stay at my house. We can't be out here now. It's too dangerous."

It was too late. An army of skeletons marched through town, striking anyone who was in their path.

Zombies followed the skeletons; the vacant-eyed mob ripped doors from their hinges, forcing the townspeople to flee from their homes.

Lily checked her inventory. She had enough potions and arrows. Lily sprinted toward the skeleton army with her diamond sword and slammed it against as many skeletons as she could hit.

Robin splashed potions on the skeletons, weakening them, as Lily destroyed the weakened skeletons with her diamond sword.

"We make a good team," Lily told Robin.

"I wish we didn't have to fight," Robin remarked as she grabbed another potion and splattered it across the skeleton army.

Lily felt confident they could defeat the bony mobs and the vacant-eyed zombies, but she faltered when she saw the sky fill with blazes and ghasts.

Warren and Simon used their fists and arrows to defeat the flying Nether mobs one by one, but they were outnumbered. A townsperson fought alongside Warren and Simon, but she was hit by a fireball and destroyed.

"I hope she respawns." Lily could barely speak, she was so scared that her friends might be struck by a fireball and destroyed.

"We have to defeat these skeletons and zombies so we can help them," Robin called to Lily.

Michael joined Lily and Robin in their battle against the mobs of the Overworld. But as he looked at the ground, he shouted, "Mr. Anarchy's summoned endermites!"

Endermites crawled on the ground of Lisimi Village. Michael struck the small, powerful insects with his diamond sword. The endermites that were biting his legs were spawning Endermen. Michael ran into the water to get away from the lanky mobs that let out piercing shrieks.

Michael emerged from the water and was immediately struck by a fireball.

"Drink milk," Lily called out to Michael. "You don't want to be destroyed by a Nether mob—you might not respawn!"

A few more townspeople joined Lily and Robin in their battle. Lily was happy to see she had help. She was exhausted and could barely strike another skeleton.

"I just wish it was daylight!" Robin looked up at the sky. She wished she could make the night pass quickly, but she was too busy battling the mobs to use her command blocks—and besides, they were too precious to use lightly, even in such an intense battle.

Warren and Simon tirelessly shot arrows at the ghasts and used their fists to redirect the blazes' fireballs back toward the flying beasts.

Warren had only a few hearts left. He tried to dodge the blasts from the fireballs and grab some milk, but he couldn't; the numerous fireballs that flew toward him overwhelmed him.

Lily sprinted to Warren and gave him some milk. She feared the powerful Nether mobs.

A fireball flew toward Lily, and she used her fist to destroy the blaze. She watched as more townspeople flocked to the shoreline to battle these mobs. Lily had an idea.

"Does anyone have a potion of water breathing?"

Ilana the Alchemist dashed toward Lily. "I do! And I have a lot!"

"Everyone," Lily called out to the folks batting the mobs, "we can escape by jumping in the water. Let's meet at the shoreline. Ilana the Alchemist has a potion of water breathing."

"Don't worry, you don't have to trade anything for the potion. Just take it. I want save everyone," Ilana offered generously.

The townspeople shielded themselves from the mobs and sprinted toward the water, drinking the potion of water breathing. Lily was the last person to drink the potion. She jumped into the refreshing blue water and swam deep underneath the ocean. Lily felt safe. She looked over to see the townspeople swimming next to her. She wondered how long they could stay under the water; she hoped they could stay there until morning. Once it was daylight, the mobs of the Overworld would disappear. They would only be left to battle Mr. Anarchy's Nether and End mobs, and they could focus their full attention on surviving the dangerous fight.

Michael, Warren, Simon, and Robin swam toward Lily. Michael called out, "I see an ocean monument."

Lily cried, "I see a guardian."

It was too late to battle the guardian. It had already struck Lily and she was hit with Mining Fatigue. She couldn't move. She thought she was losing her final heart and was panicked that she'd respawn in the thick of the battle at Lisimi Village—or, worse, that she might not respawn at all.

Lily was shocked when she saw someone swim toward her and hand her some milk.

"Leon?" Lily asked as she sipped the milk. "What are you doing here?'

13
SUMMONING A STORM

"Mr. Anarchy didn't destroy me with his Nether mob," Leon tried to explain, but he was distracted when another gray guardian swam toward him.

"We have to swim," Lily exclaimed.

Lily and Leon swam away from the guardian and toward the ocean monument, avoiding blasts from the hostile fish and entering the grand underwater temple.

"Lily!" Michael called out. He was busy battling an elder guardian. Lily charged toward the powerful elder guardian and struck it with her diamond sword, slamming her sword into the side of the fish.

When the fish was destroyed, they swam further into the monument, wondering if they might find gold blocks inside. Lily always loved being under the water, and she was surprised how easy it was to swim in this deep blue ocean while navigating her way through the monument. The water felt calming and the monument was peaceful, despite the presence of hostile mobs.

"Gold blocks!" Simon called as they swam toward him.

Warren spotted Leon swimming alongside Lily. "What are you doing here?" Warren struck Leon with his diamond sword.

"Stop!" Lily cried. "Leon helped me."

"Helped you?" Warren couldn't believe Lily was defending Leon.

"Yes, he gave me milk when I thought I was about to be destroyed."

Michael said, "He's not getting any gold blocks."

Warren picked up the gold blocks and filled his inventory. He handed them to his friends, but they didn't give blocks to Leon.

"I can explain." Leon wanted to clear his name.

"We don't care," Michael said and swam out of the monument. As Lily swam behind her friend Michael, she saw the other townspeople swimming to the surface.

A townsperson called out, "It's daylight."

Everyone rushed to the surface and swam to the shoreline. There were still a handful of blazes and ghasts floating in the sky. Lily and her friends aimed bows and arrows at the Nether mobs and destroyed them, but there was no time to celebrate their victory. Just as the last mob disappeared from the sky, the sound of thunder boomed throughout the town.

"A rainstorm!" Michael exclaimed. Thunder crashed again, and a single bolt of lightning shot through the sky. Leon was opening his mouth to defend himself again when the bolt struck him, erasing him from town. With a final groan of thunder, the short rainstorm fizzled out and left the townspeople wondering at Leon's sudden disappearance.

"Where did he go?" asked Robin.

"I assume he went back home." Lily looked over at the space where Leon had just stood. She had never heard Leon's explanation, but she knew that he had saved her from battling the hostile mobs on her own in the water.

Michael and the others muttered that they were happy he was gone, but they also added that they were jealous. Tensions in the town were running high, and everyone wanted to go back home.

Lily stood by the remnants of her home. Wolfie barked and ran by the large hole where her small cottage once stood.

"I used to wish I could spend my entire day playing Minecraft, and now I just want to leave and go home and play outside with my friends." Tears filled Lily's eyes.

"You don't mean that. You just want to leave this server." Simon knew Lily was one of the biggest Minecraft fans.

"Help me rebuild." She scoured her inventory for supplies to rebuild the cottage, but she didn't have enough resources.

Robin offered her a few wooden planks and said, "We have to find out if Mr. Anarchy or the person in the green jumpsuit destroyed your house. It would be a shame to rebuild it, just to have it blown up again."

Michael added, "What about Leon? He could have destroyed your home, too."

"We have way too many suspects." Lily's head was spinning. She hated all of these distractions. Weren't they supposed to focus on finding their way home? Weren't they supposed to summon a storm?

"I know we have a lot of suspects, but we still have to figure out who did this," Robin said as she poked through her inventory searching for more supplies for Lily's cottage.

Lily looked at Warren. "Let's have that town meeting now."

"Okay." Warren nodded. "Good idea. We should host it now that we are free from hostile mobs."

The group called all of the townspeople into the center of town. Juan the Butcher, Fred the Farmer, and Emily the Fisherwoman joined the meeting. Warren addressed the small crowd. "Everyone did a fantastic job battling the hostile mobs of both the Overworld and the Nether. Now we need to focus on our plan for getting home. Does anyone have a new idea?"

Lily interrupted, "No need for new ideas! I am going to summon a storm."

"How?" Warren asked, and the townspeople murmured to each other questioningly.

"I have command blocks!" Lily said, digging in her inventory. She unearthed one of the multicolored blocks and presented it to the cheering crowd.

14
REBUILD AND RETALIATE

As the clapping and cheers roared all around her, Lily placed the command block on the ground. "We don't know exactly how accurate this lightning bolt will be," she called, "so whoever it strikes is the lucky person who will get to go home. We hope we have enough for everyone to use."

With that, she used the command block to summon a lightning bolt. It hovered in the air for a moment, gathering more electricity and growing more powerful. Then it flashed toward the ground, striking a townsperson with a brilliant flash.

But when Lily's eyes adjusted again after the bright light, the townsperson was still standing in the spot they were struck in. The crowd and Lily's friends gasped, clearly realizing just what she had—the command block hadn't worked.

"What?" Lily called out in anger.

A voice rose through the crowd. "It's not as easy as you think."

Lily looked up and saw Mr. Anarchy stepping out of the assembled group.

Lily leapt at him, but he splashed a potion on himself and disappeared.

Warren sighed. "Okay, so the command blocks didn't work. We can't give up. Does anyone else have any ideas for escaping the Overworld?"

But just then, a townsperson dressed in a red sweater called out, "Over there! There's the Prismarine!"

Lily ran toward the Prismarine, cornering him by the large roller coaster. She turned around to see the entire town crowded behind her.

"What do you want?" The man in the green jumpsuit cowered.

"Who are you?" Lily asked.

He shook as he responded, "I'm Matthew."

"Why are you dressed like one of the Prismarines?" Michael asked.

"Because I am one. Or, well, I was one. I escaped, but recently I was invited to participate in a Minecraft Olympics competition, and I didn't realize it was on this server. I joined, and then I was zapped back in. When I arrived here, I felt like it was all a bad dream. I didn't want to be here. Now I am just hoping that I'll be struck by lightning or that Brett and Greta will notice I'm missing and try to save me."

"You know Brett and Greta?" Lily's heart skipped a beat. She missed her friends dearly and wanted any information about them.

"Yes." He sighed. "I do know them."

"Can they actually rescue you?" asked Lily.

"I don't know. I hope so," Matthew explained.

"Mr. Anarchy is awful," Lily shook her head. "We have to stop him."

"I'm not so sure this is the work of Mr. Anarchy. It sounds like Leon is behind this," Robin said.

Lily wondered if Robin was right. How could they be sure that Matthew was telling the truth? "But Leon was working with Mr. Anarchy, and recruiting players to replace him on Mr. Anarchy's team." She narrowed her eyes at Matthew. "You've been back on the server a long time, and we've hardly seen you. Have you been working with Mr. Anarchy, just like Leon?"

"N-no," Matthew said. "I swear!"

"Come on, Lily," Simon said. "If he's a Prismarine, he's a friend. We can't let Mr. Anarchy keep us from trusting our friends."

Michael nodded. "So, if you escaped, does that mean that all of your friends are still in the real world?" he asked.

"I guess so." Matthew took a deep breath and wiped the tears from his eyes. "I never wanted to be back here. I just want to leave. Can you summon a lightning bolt?"

"I wish it was that easy. I summoned one earlier and it didn't get us anywhere. I want to go home, too," explained Lily with a sigh. Her friends were right— how could she not trust Matthew?

"The one cool thing is that once you get zapped back into the real world, it's like you never left. I was zapped back into the same point in time that I was trapped on the server. My parents didn't know I was gone."

Lily was relieved to hear this, because she had spent a lot of time worrying about her parents and how upset they must be because she was missing.

"I guess that means we aren't missing that math test," Simon joked. "That was the only good thing about being trapped here."

"Seriously?" Lily asked Simon.

"You know how bad I am at long division!" Simon defended himself. "And Mrs. Sanders was about to give me detention for passing notes in class."

Although Matthew had brought them good news, Lily still wanted to find a way home. But she also realized something else. "If Matthew and Leon weren't responsible for destroying my house and arranging these attacks, we only have one suspect."

"Yes," Michael agreed. "It has to be Mr. Anarchy."

"We still don't know how to get home, but we can't wait for Mr. Anarchy to destroy more homes and send Nether mobs to attack us and erase us from the Overworld," Warren said. "I think we should look for Mr. Anarchy."

"Yes," Lily said. "It's time to settle this, once and for all."

The townspeople agreed, and they followed Lily and her friends out of town and to the hole housing the minecarts. The friends and villagers piled into the carts and traveled to the jungle biome.

"This is Mr. Anarchy's house," Lily told the townspeople.

Matthew shuddered when he saw the temple. "I was trapped in here for so long. I can't go back here."

Ilana said, "Why don't we douse ourselves with potions of invisibility? Then we'll be able to search for Mr. Anarchy without his army trapping us."

"That's a good idea," Lily remarked. "But I don't think we have to do that."

Michael walked closer to the jungle temple and asked, "Where are the blue griefers?"

"You noticed that, too?" Lily said.

Simon ran into the jungle temple and cried out, "It's empty!"

15
CEASEFIRE

"Where's Mr. Anarchy?" Lily wondered aloud as she explored his empty jungle temple.

Robin called out, "The command blocks are missing."

Michael added, "I bet he relocated."

"Do we have to look for him?" Matthew asked.

Simon looked around the barren temple and remarked, "I think this is a trap. He knew we would come here to battle him."

"Do you think he found a way out of here?" Lily mused. "Maybe he's back in the real world."

"I don't think so," Michael said. "But that is a possibility."

Lily remembered Leon telling them about a room where a team of players were working on helping Mr. Anarchy escape from the server. She rushed down the hall in search of the room. She hoped Mr. Anarchy had left these people behind—it seemed like the sort of thing he'd do. Lily searched for a room like the one Leon had described, but she couldn't find one.

"Remember Leon told us about that room where Mr. Anarchy had his team of players that worked to get him off this server?"

"Yes," replied Michael.

"I don't see a room like that anywhere in this temple!" Lily had searched the entire temple and there wasn't a door to open.

"I wonder if Leon was making that up," said Michael.

Lily noticed a piece of redstone dust on the ground. "What's this?"

She walked over and banged her pickaxe against the floor. Pieces crumbled at her feet. She called the others over. "Look what I found."

"It's a button. Should we press it?" asked Michael.

Lily nodded and, after hesitating for only a moment, she pressed the button on the floor, activating pistons that were in a piston door. They looked up and saw a secret stronghold.

"Wow," Simon marveled.

"Shhh!" Lily warned him. "I bet Mr. Anarchy is hiding down here."

They walked into the stronghold together. Lily placed a torch on the wall and explored the dark and musty room. A skeleton spawned in the corner of the dimly-lit room.

"Watch out!" Simon cried to Lily.

Suddenly, an army of blue griefers stormed toward them. They held diamond swords and leapt at the group.

"You weren't gone. You were just hiding!" Lily exclaimed, lunging at a blue griefer.

Mr. Anarchy called to them, "It took you long enough. I wondered if you'd ever find us."

"What do you want from us?" Lily yelled. "Isn't it bad enough that you've trapped us on this server? Now you want to torture us, too?"

Michael cried out, "We want a ceasefire."

"A ceasefire?" Mr. Anarchy was curious. He motioned to his soldiers to lower their weapons, and Lily and her friends did the same. Everyone looked at Michael.

Michael explained, "We all want the same thing. We want to leave this server in the Overworld. Can't we work together to find a way out of here? Why are you busy battling us? It doesn't make any sense."

Before Mr. Anarchy could answer, Robin cried, "Look down!"

Silverfish crawled on the floor of the stronghold. Everyone slammed their diamond swords against the small insects.

The ceasefire seemed to be over almost as quickly as it began. "Did you spawn these silverfish?" Lily held her sword against Mr. Anarchy's chest.

Mr. Anarchy looked down at the silverfish crowding around his feet. "No," he stammered.

Four block-carrying Endermen walked into the stronghold. One of them shrieked and teleported toward Mr. Anarchy as the griefer stood frozen in terror.

"Help! How can I destroy this mob?" he cried out. He struck the lanky mob with his diamond sword, but his energy was low. With a last strike from the Enderman, Mr. Anarchy was destroyed.

The blue griefers seemed furious; they flooded the gang with arrows. Their aggressive attack weakened the gang and destroyed a handful of townspeople. Lily hoped her theory that only Nether and End mobs destroyed players for good was correct and that their friends would respawn back in the village.

Warren called for help. "I need milk! I'm losing energy."

Lily sprinted to her friend's side, but it was too late. Warren was destroyed.

Frantic, Lily ran away from the battle, dashing to the mineshaft and taking a minecart back into town. She had to know if Warren had respawned in the village. Her heart was racing as she leapt out of her minecart and ran the rest of the way.

The town was eerily empty. The Nether mobs had vanished. Then Lily heard a shout.

Lily sprinted in the direction of the sound. Warren stood in the center of the village, next to a pile of rubble that was once the town library.

She gasped when she saw Mr. Anarchy pointing his diamond sword at Warren.

"Do you know who is behind these Nether and End attacks?" Mr. Anarchy asked.

"No." Warren's voice was weak. His energy was still depleted.

Lily sprinted over, grabbing a potion as she ran. "I swear I will splash this on you. Don't play games with us, Mr. Anarchy. We know you're responsible for these attacks."

"I'm not," Mr. Anarchy insisted. "Splash all you want. I'll just respawn, and the attacks won't end."

Lily hesitated, looking closely at Mr. Anarchy's face. He was sweating and pale. He actually looked desperate to know where the attacks were coming from. Could he be telling the truth? Lily bit her lip and made a decision; she put the potion back in her inventory. "You weren't hiding from us, were you? You were hiding from someone else."

Mr. Anarchy nodded, and at that moment, Michael ran out of his house, where Lily guessed he had just respawned. "Don't worry about a ceasefire with Mr. Anarchy," Michael called out to the group. "He's not the person we're fighting. There's someone more sinister on this server."

"I promise to honor our ceasefire and work with you to stop whoever is terrorizing the server," said Mr. Anarchy.

Lily was skeptical. "Are you telling us the truth? If we worked together, we'd be extremely powerful. We could beat any griefer on this server."

Mr. Anarchy replied, "It's not what I want, but it's what we have to do. If we don't team up, we'll all be destroyed."

But Lily didn't have a chance to contemplate this partnership; just then, a Wither and an Ender Dragon spawned in the sky above them.

Mr. Anarchy struck the side of the scaly dragon, but it struck back with a roar. Mr. Anarchy shot a frightened look at the group, but he seemed to decide to save himself. Reaching into his inventory, he pulled out a potion of invisibility and splashed it on himself, escaping.

16
TRY AGAIN

"**H**ow we can battle these beasts?" Lily cried. "We need more people than just the three of us— but all of our friends are still in the jungle."

She was proven wrong when four blue soldiers ran into town from the direction of the minecarts. "Do you want this to end?" their leader called.

"The attacks?" asked Lily as she pounded her sword against the Ender Dragon's powerful wing.

"We can stop them," the blue griefer told them.

Another griefer said, "We don't want to attack you."

The four griefers were extremely skilled fighters, and they sprinted through the town, defeating the Ender Dragon and the Wither on their own.

"How did you do that?" Lily was impressed.

"Mr. Anarchy recruited us due to our fighting skills," a griefer replied.

Lily remembered that that was why Mr. Anarchy had made Leon recruit Robin. She wondered if Robin and her other friends were okay in the jungle temple. Mr. Anarchy had probably respawned there, and he might be attacking them. She didn't know if she trusted his offer of a truce after he had left them to fight the boss mobs on their own.

The blue griefer spoke, and Lily was jolted back to reality. He confessed, "We are staging an uprising. We're the ones who are summoning the Nether and End mobs, and we tweaked the game so that when our mobs destroy players, they don't respawn. Our hope was to destroy Mr. Anarchy once and for all, but the change may be working differently. We believe that some of these attacks have helped people get back to the real world. We also want to overthrow Mr. Anarchy."

Lily gasped.

"That's why he asked to work with us," Michael remarked.

"You can bet we won't work with him now," Lily agreed.

"We've been attacking him however we can, and he's growing weaker. We don't want him terrorizing this server. We all want to find our way home," another griefer added.

Lily was thrilled. They had a new group of people to work with in their battle against Mr. Anarchy. Now that Mr. Anarchy had lost his powerful army and didn't have any minions, he'd be extremely vulnerable.

"We will work with you," Lily told the blue griefers.

"I'm not so sure, Lily," Michael said. He turned to the blue griefers. "Do you know who blew up Lily's cottage?"

"Matthew did," the blue griefer replied. "But before you get mad at him, you should know that he didn't want to do it. Mr. Anarchy forced him. He threatened to put him on Hardcore mode. Matthew was so upset that he was back on this server that he followed Mr. Anarchy's orders."

"Please don't blame Matthew for this," pleaded another blue griefer.

Lily's head was spinning. She couldn't process all of this. It seemed so sudden. Just when she had agreed to trust Matthew, he'd lied to her. And now here they were, standing in the center of an empty Lisimi Village, making an alliance with Mr. Anarchy's army.

Robin ran toward them. "Guys!"

"Robin!" Lily was excited to be reunited with her friend. "How are the others?"

"They're fine. We're working with the blue griefers. We are going to destroy Mr. Anarchy."

"These blue griefers also want to help destroy Mr. Anarchy." Lily introduced Robin to the four blue griefers that stood next to her.

"I think we finally have a chance of defeating him." Robin was hopeful.

"We have to go back to the jungle temple," a blue griefer informed them.

"Let's hop in the minecarts," suggested Robin.

"No need," one of the griefers said with a smile. "We can TP."

Another griefer added, "This is Mike, the best hacker in the Overworld. He can override anything Mr. Anarchy does to us."

The friends grinned.

"I'll also stop summoning the Nether and End mobs, and send them back to where they belong," Mike said. "And I'll turn off their ability to keep players from respawning, just in case it's hurting people."

With a nod to each other, the gang TPed back to the jungle biome.

When Simon saw his friends, he dashed out of the jungle temple, grinning. "We've trapped Mr. Anarchy!"

17
GOODBYE, MR. ANARCHY

Lily ran into the jungle temple. Matthew called out to her. "We have him trapped in a prison cell."

"Great," Lily replied. She wanted to confront Matthew about the fact that he blew up her cottage, but she knew it wasn't his fault. They were in this battle together. She opened the door to the prison.

"Lily, my friend!" Mr. Anarchy was weak but he tried to smile slyly.

"Don't you dare call me a friend," Lily replied. "You lied to us, again. You did this to yourself," Lily said, gesturing to the cell around him.

Michael entered the small prison cell. "Now it's our turn to spawn mobs and watch you battle them. Is there still a hole in the ceiling of the prison?"

Mr. Anarchy didn't reply.

"Being trapped in a prison isn't much fun, is it?" Lily pointed her diamond sword at the sinister master griefer.

Again, Mr. Anarchy said nothing.

"Well, the game is over." Michael splashed a potion of harming on Mr. Anarchy, instantly weakening him.

"You only have one heart left," said Lily.

"Go ahead and destroy me. Maybe I'll respawn in the real world."

"I doubt that," Lily replied. "And we aren't going to destroy you."

The blue griefers crammed into the small prison. One of the griefers called out, "We are so glad you're in prison. You've trapped us on this server. We are all going to find a way to get off this server, but we will be sure to leave you behind. You don't deserve to return to the real world."

One by one, the blue griefers began to change their skins, and then one ex-griefer asked the townspeople, "Can we live in Lisimi Village with you?"

Another blue griefer, who was now a regular player dressed in jeans and a t-shirt, said, "We can put together an elite team that helps to plot ways of getting off this server."

Michael smiled. "That sounds like a good idea, right, guys?"

The townspeople cheered.

Mr. Anarchy called out in a weak voice, "Are you going to leave me here in the jungle temple?"

"No," Warren remarked. "We don't trust you. You're coming back to Lisimi Village. You will help us rebuild, and we will make sure you don't wreak any more havoc on this server."

The group left the jungle temple and started on their journey back to Lisimi Village.

Lily remarked, "We have to hurry back to the village. It's almost nighttime."

"You don't want to get destroyed by hostile mobs," Mr. Anarchy said with a hint of a laugh.

Lily poked Mr. Anarchy with her diamond sword, "We don't want to hear anything from you. You've caused enough damage."

It was getting dark when they approached the town. Lily realized she didn't have a place to spend the night. "I don't have a house," she said.

Matthew walked over to Lily. "I want to apologize. I'm the one who blew up your house, but I didn't want to do it. I pleaded with Mr. Anarchy not to make me do something so cruel to you. But in the end, I did it, and I accept responsibility."

Lily looked at Mr. Anarchy. "How could you force someone to blow up my cottage? I loved that place."

"You can't force anyone to blow up a house. It was his choice," Mr. Anarchy defended himself.

"But you told me that you'd put me on Hardcore mode." Matthew was angry.

"You are easy to manipulate," Mr. Anarchy said, laughing.

"Let's not pay attention to Mr. Anarchy," announced Lily. "He doesn't deserve our time." She looked over at Matthew. "I forgive you. But you're going to have to help me rebuild the cottage."

"I promise, I will rebuild it."

Juan the Butcher walked over to them. "Welcome home!"

Warren introduced Juan to the new residents of Lisimi Village. "We have these new people coming to live here, but they don't have a place to stay."

Juan replied, "I've kept track of the people who haven't respawned. You can have them stay in those people's homes."

Everyone found a new place to live. Mr. Anarchy went home with Warren, who was going to keep an eye on him.

"If you try to escape, we will find you," Warren threatened Mr. Anarchy. "You have no army. You're helpless."

Mr. Anarchy had no response. He seemed to be deep in thought.

Lily and Robin spent the night in a small brick house. As Lily crawled into bed, she called out to Robin, "Soon I'll have my cottage rebuilt, and you can come live with me."

"That's so nice," Robin replied.

"We're going to make the best of being trapped here," said Lily.

"Do you think we can ride that roller coaster tomorrow?" asked Robin.

"Of course. But that's just one ride on a coaster. We have do something better to celebrate the end of Mr. Anarchy's reign of terror. Let's plan a big party. We can invite everyone from Lisimi Village."

Robin smiled. "That sounds like a plan."

Lily drifted off to sleep and dreamed about the big party.

18
CELEBRATIONS

"**W**hat yummy cake," Robin remarked as the town gathered to celebrate Mr. Anarchy being captured.

Michael looked up at the sky. "I love seeing a clear sky. There are no hostile mobs from the Nether and the End terrorizing us today. All I see is clouds."

Lily said, "I like my view, too." She was looking off into the distance, where Mr. Anarchy and Matthew were busy building her a new cottage.

Juan the Butcher offered the townspeople fresh chicken and beef. Everyone thanked him and feasted. Emily the Fisherwoman walked into the center of the village with fresh fish to add to the table.

"I've never eaten this much in my life. This is truly decadent." Robin smiled as she devoured a plate of fish.

Fred the Farmer gathered a bunch of crops and placed them on the table in the center of the village. "Please help yourself to apples and potatoes."

There was a festive vibe, and everyone was excited to spend the day celebrating in the peaceful Overworld. Although the entire town longed to return to the real world, they were going to enjoy their time on the server.

Matthew walked over and told Lily, "I think you'll be able to stay in the cottage tonight."

Lily grinned, thrilled at the thought of being back in her cottage. She could hear Wolfie barking nearby.

Michael approached Lily. "I have an idea. I think we should go on a treasure hunt."

"A treasure hunt?" Simon sprinted over. "I love treasure hunts."

"That sounds like fun," Lily replied.

"Can I go with you?" asked Matthew.

"Of course," Lily said.

As they ate the last pieces of cake, the gang planned their next adventure.

Check out the rest of the
Unofficial Minetrapped Adventure series
and read what happens to Simon, Lily, and Michael:

Trapped in the
Overworld
WINTER MORGAN

Mobs in the
Mine
WINTER MORGAN

Terror on a
Treasure Hunt
WINTER MORGAN

Ghastly Battle
WINTER MORGAN

Creeper Invasion
WINTER MORGAN

Attack of the
Ender Dragon
WINTER MORGAN

Available wherever books are sold!

DO YOU LIKE FICTION FOR MINECRAFTERS?

Check out other unofficial Minecrafter adventures from Sky Pony Press!

Invasion of the Overworld
MARK CHEVERTON

Battle for the Nether
MARK CHEVERTON

Confronting the Dragon
MARK CHEVERTON

Trouble in Zombie-town
MARK CHEVERTON

The Quest for the Diamond Sword
WINTER MORGAN

The Mystery of the Griefer's Mark
WINTER MORGAN

The Endermen Invasion
WINTER MORGAN

Treasure Hunters in Trouble
WINTER MORGAN

Available wherever books are sold!

LIKE OUR BOOKS FOR MINECRAFTERS?

Then check out other novels by Sky Pony Press.

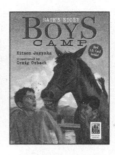

Pack of Dorks
BETH VRABEL

Boys Camp: Zack's Story
CAMERON DOKEY, CRAIG ORBACK

Boys Camp: Nate's Story
KITSON JAZYNKA, CRAIG ORBACK

Letters from an Alien Schoolboy
R. L. ASQUITH

Just a Drop of Water
KERRY O'MALLEY CERRA

Future Flash
KITA HELMETAG MURDOCK

Sky Run
ALEX SHEARER

Mr. Big
CAROL AND MATT DEMBICKI

Available wherever books are sold!